CW01216851

Dr. Madeleine Vieira's Anxiety Disorder Series
I'M AFRAID

Obsessive-Compulsive Disorder

Khloe Kitten
IS AFRAID OF GERMS!

Illustrated by Oxana Fomina

Copyright © 2023 Dr. Madeleine Vieira
All rights reserved

The right of Dr. Madeleine Vieira to be identified as the author of this work has been asserted in accordance with Section 78 of the Copyright, Designs and Patents Act 1988. The book cover is Copyright to Dr. Madeleine Vieira.

Grosvenor House Publishing Ltd - Link House, 140 The Broadway, Tolworth, Surrey, KT6 7HT
www.grosvenorhousepublishing.co.uk

This book is sold subject to the conditions that it shall not, by way of trade or otherwise, be lent, resold, hired out or otherwise circulated without the author's or publisher's prior consent in any form of binding or cover other than that in which it is published and without a similar condition including this condition being imposed on the subsequent purchaser.

The book is a book of fiction. Any resemblance to people or events, past or present, is purely coincidental.
A CIP record for this book is available from the British Library.

ISBN 978-1-80381-399-8

This book is dedicated to my husband Christophe
and daughters Allegra, Alexia-Amalia and Eleonora,
with all my love,
and to children worldwide suffering from
Obsessive-Compulsive Disorder.

Dr. Madeleine Vieira's *I'M AFRAID* book focusing on Obsessive-Compulsive Disorder has been written with the intent to help children suffering from this disorder. She would like to note that although therapeutic children's books are a valuable and much-needed resource, they are not a replacement for in-person therapeutic treatment with a mental health professional.

While Dr. Vieira strives to help children overcome symptoms of anxiety through her series, she shall not be held liable for any content in this or any of her therapeutic children's books.

Introduction to Parents and Caregivers

Dear Parents and Caregivers,

It's easy to understand how difficult it is for parents and caregivers of a child with anxiety to cope with the situation. Their child's fear comes with an array of symptoms, such as a rapid heartbeat, dizziness, headaches, stomachaches, shaking, and trouble breathing. The child will go to great lengths to avoid triggers that bring these feelings on.

As parents and caregivers are a child's champion, you want to protect your child from these unpleasant and sometimes overwhelming symptoms.

You try to reassure your child. You try to help your child. You use logic and even allow your child to avoid the distressing situations.

Nothing works.

You may become frustrated and even angry at times as your child's anxiety controls his life and yours. You can't understand why seemingly ordinary situations frighten him.

If not addressed, your child's anxiety can worsen. He may not be able to go to school or have normal social relationships.

There is good news though! It is possible for children to overcome their anxiety. Through diligence and positive thinking children with anxiety can lead healthy and happy lives.

Based on the therapeutic technique of Exposure Response Prevention (ERP), a component of Cognitive Behavioral Therapy (CBT), *Khloe Kitten Is Afraid of Germs!* demonstrates that it is possible for children to manage their anxiety. The story guides children through steps that research shows help them overcome the harmful habits and patterns they've developed while struggling with their fears. Along with the story, there is an About Anxiety page, a Coping Strategies page, and a Stepladder page. These additional tools can help alleviate anxiety symptoms.

If anxiety interferes with your child's life, please consult a mental health professional. Working in collaboration with a professional and letting your child know that you're confident he will be successful will give your child a stronger foundation and allow him to become his own champion fear fighter.

Warmest Wishes,
Dr. Madeleine Vieira

"Hi, Khloe," called Pablo Parrot. "Come play with us."

Charlie Cub zipped down a large tube slide. "Weeeee!"

Khloe Kitten's heart began to race as she watched them touch the dirty slide.

"Maybe later." Khloe moved far away from the slide. She wiped off the seat five times and whispered, "It's okay," three times before sitting down.

"Boy, I wish I could go down that slide," she mumbled. But she couldn't stop thinking something bad would happen if she got dirty.

"Hello, Khloe," said Ollie. "I noticed you aren't playing with the others and you cleaned off the seat before sitting down. Are you perhaps having worry thoughts that you're trying to get rid of?"

Khloe lowered her head. "Y-Yes. It stops me from doing things. If I have to touch something I think is germy, I'm so afraid, my heart races. I need to clean it over and over. Then after touching it, I have to wash my paws and change my clothes. And, I have to tell myself everything is okay three times."

"I see that your paws are raw from washing them too much," said Ollie, adjusting his monocle. "They must hurt. You know, I help children who have problems like yours. What if I help you as well?"

"Uh ... I'm not sure," said Khloe. "What do I have to do?"

"First thing," said Ollie, "it's important to understand that you don't have to do what these thoughts and fears keep telling you to do. These worries are trying to bully you, and you can stand up to bully thoughts and say, NO."

"Hmm," said Khloe, "I never thought of it like that. What should I do instead?"

"Well," said Ollie, "Instead of obeying bully thoughts, you would need to do the opposite of what they're telling you to do. By going against what the bully thoughts are telling you, your brain will learn to stop listening to them. You can face your fear by going down the slide without doing the ritual of cleaning and telling yourself, it's okay. If you do that over and over, eventually this will become your natural way of responding to bully thoughts."

A shiver raced down Khloe's back as she watched her friends shoot out of the tube slide.
"It's full of germs, but I'll try. I really want to go down that slide."

"Excellent," said Ollie. "One way to overcome a big fear is to face smaller fears first. Then slowly work your way up to the big fear in baby steps. Each fear you face is a little more difficult than the one before. Think of climbing a ladder, each step helps you slowly reach your goal."

"Are there a lot of steps?" Khloe asked.

The number of steps varies," said Ollie. "You can try as many as you like. How about trying six and see how it goes? The main thing is to repeat each step until it doesn't bother you as much."

Khloe's face lit up. "I think I can do that! Tonight, I'll think of my first step."

"Morning, Ollie. I decided on my first step! I'm going to try to sit on that bench ... without cleaning it first."

"Good one," said Ollie.

The kitten sat down but hopped right off. She then quickly cleaned herself with wipes and kept telling herself, *it's okay.*

"Sorry, Ollie. I can't do it."

"Try again," said Ollie. "Tell yourself you CAN do it."

It's okay. It's okay. It's okay.

Khloe squirmed on the bench. "I feel too dirty. I need to change my clothes and wash myself."

"I know it's uncomfortable," said Ollie, "but what if you handle this for just five minutes then you can move away. It's important you don't wash yourself or change your clothes after you move away."

"Oh, no." Khloe's whiskers drooped. "O-Okay."

After five minutes, Khloe jumped up and brushed her clothes off. "I have to go home to change." She began to tell herself, *it's okay.*

Ollie tilted his head. "You could do that, but it might be helpful if you talk back to your bully thoughts. It will help you feel stronger."

"BULLY THOUGHTS, you might make me uncomfortable but you can't make me clean myself," said Khloe.

"Well done, Khloe! I know it feels uncomfortable, but it's important to stop the habit of cleaning yourself and telling yourself 'it's okay' every time you touch something you think is dirty."

Ollie gave Khloe a piece of dried chicken. "Rewarding yourself for each step you try helps build confidence."

"Thanks, Ollie. Oh, can I wash my paws before meals?"

"Washing your paws one time before meals and changing your clothes before bed is fine. Just make sure you aren't washing more than once or doing any rituals when you wash and change clothes."

"That was hard. I was shaking, but I'm glad I did it."
Khloe practiced until she felt comfortable sitting on the bench.

"You're doing great," said Ollie. "Tonight, try to think of Step 2."

"Morning, Ollie. I can't think of anything for Step 2."

Ollie tapped his chin. "Hmm, what if we go to the market and you touch some items?"

"I guess I'll try. The food there is mostly clean, but other people might have touched it, so it might have germs," said Khloe.

"Hi!" yelled Sophia Swan, racing up to them. "I'll come!"

Khloe tried to touch the bread, but her heart raced. Then she tried to touch some apples, but her stomach did flip-flops. *They're full of germs,* she thought. *I'll have to clean my paws.*

"Those apples look good," said Sophia. She leaned over to get one and knocked the kitten right into them.

"AAHHHHHH!" Khloe rushed away then pulled out a wipe and cleaned herself.

"Sorry!" called Sophia.

"Are you okay?" asked Ollie.

"I'm a failure."

"Pish-posh!" said Ollie. "It takes time to overcome a fear. Even trying a step should be rewarded. You can also take slow, deep breaths to help calm yourself. And, remind yourself that you're strong enough to stand feeling uncomfortable. The discomfort goes away with time."

Khloe stared at the apples. "I'm going to try again." She took a couple of breaths and reached for the apples.

"Wonderful," said Ollie.

"This is a lot harder than I thought," said Khloe. "My legs felt weak, but I'm happy I did it."

"What if you play a game as a reward?" suggested Ollie.

"I'll play with you," said Sophia.

A weak smile crept across Khloe's face. "I'd like that. I'll practice Step 2 after that."

Ollie joined Khloe in the school playground the next day.

"What if I climb the monkey bars for Step 3? This step is harder because I know other kids have touched them."

"That's an excellent step," said Ollie.

Khloe looked at the monkey bars.
Her head and belly ached. *All the other
kids' germs are on those bars*, she thought.

She took a few slow, deep breaths and told
herself, *GO AWAY BULLY THOUGHTS.*

She put one paw on the bar then the other.
"I can do this," she repeated as she climbed up.

"Great job!" yelled her friends.
They raced to Khloe.

"Thanks," said Khloe. "It was scary, and I want to clean my paws and change clothes, but I'm not going to. I'm proud of myself for overcoming Step 3."

"I'm proud of you too," said Ollie. "What about a reward?"

"I'll draw a picture with my new coloring pencils. After I practice Step 3, I'll think about Step 4."

The next day, Khloe met Ollie in the park. "I couldn't think of anything for Step 4. Everything seems too scary."

"What if you try to touch the bathroom door?" asked Ollie.

Khloe's tail slung between her legs. "I-I don't know. But I'll try."

She stretched out her paw to touch the door, but stopped. "This is harder than the last step. My legs feel like jelly. It's too germy to touch."

"Do your breathing," said Ollie. "And talk back to your fear and bully thoughts."

"O-Okay." *I can do this*, she kept reminding herself.

With her lips crunched tight, Khloe tried again.

"Yuck," she yelled as she touched the door. About to race to the sink to clean herself, she remembered what Ollie said. She took slow, deep breaths.

"Excellent," said Ollie.

"Way to go," cheered her friends.

Beads of sweat sat on Khloe's forehead. "I didn't think I'd be able to do it, but I did! I'll practice it some more then bake a cake with my mother as a reward."

"You're on your way," said Ollie. "How about Step 5?"

"Uh ... I'm feeling more confident, but the steps are getting a lot harder," said Khloe. "I don't think I can do any more."

Pablo put his wing on Khloe's shoulder. "Ollie, is there anything else she can do to help fight her fear?"

"There is," said Ollie. "Khloe, you can fight fear not just in what you *do*, but with how you *think*."

"How do I do that?" asked the kitten.

Ollie ruffled his feathers.
"Let me explain.
If you feel afraid and your
thoughts are telling you it's scary,
tell yourself you're strong.
Imagine yourself as a champion
fear fighter and you can accomplish
anything you set your mind to."

Khloe raised her brows. "Wow! A champion fear fighter."
She wiggled her tail. "I like that."

Ollie winked at Khloe.

"It's way scarier than the last step, but ... I-I guess for
Step 5 I'll touch the bin in the school cafeteria."

Pablo, Charlie, and Sophia stood beside Khloe. "You can do it," they said.

Khloe's head ached and her stomach did flip-flops. She wanted to run away, but instead she took a deep breath and used her courage.

She reached for the bin. "FEAR, YOU DON'T SCARE ME. I'm a champion fear fighter." Her headache eased and so did her stomach.

"You're strong," yelled Khloe's friends.

Khloe raced to Ollie. "I did it!
I had to fight hard not to wash my paws after and not tell myself
'it's okay,' but I touched the bin! I'm proud of myself." She nibbled
on the kitty treat she brought for a reward.

"You should be proud," said Ollie.
"You're achieving something HUGE.
I knew you could do it."

Khloe lowered her head.
"I really want to go down the slide for Step 6,
but it's got so many germs in it. It'll be super hard."

Ollie rubbed his chin. "Yes, it will be. But you've worked your
way here with baby steps and you've been practicing.
You *can* do it."

Shaking her head, Khloe pointed her ears back.
"I feel braver, but I still have to work hard
to fight my fear."

"That's to be expected, Khloe.
Each time you accomplish a step, your fear
weakens and you get stronger. In time,
your fear will be as tiny as an ant."

"Okay, Ollie. I'll try."

The next day, Khloe stood at the bottom of the slide while her friends raced up the ladder and zoomed down through the tube.

"Come on," shouted Charlie.

Khloe's legs felt like lead and her heart pounded. *That's the germiest thing ever,* she thought. *What if I get a horrible disease?*

Then she remembered she's a champion fear fighter. "FEAR, STOP IT. I'm stronger than bully thoughts."

Using all of her courage, Khloe climbed the ladder. She wanted to go back down, but she fought her fear.

She sat on the top, took a deep breath and slid down the tube. Then she took another deep breath. "I won't clean myself or my clothes!"

"Yay!" yelled her friends.

Khloe looked at Ollie. He gave her a thumbs up and a big smile.

A feeling of victory welled up in the kitten as she jetted to him. "I DID IT! Thanks so much, Ollie, for helping me. I really am a champion fear fighter."

About Anxiety

According to Dr. Vieira, the number of children with psychological disorders is at an all-time high and of those children with a diagnosable anxiety disorder, the majority are not receiving treatment.

Anxiety is a feeling of worry, fear, or uneasiness. It can cause a variety of physical symptoms including, rapid heartbeat, sweating, dizziness, trembling, weakness, and agitation. It can often affect the quality of the sufferer's life.

While this may sound concerning, there are strategies that can be used to help manage a child's anxiety symptoms.

Cognitive Behavioral Therapy (CBT) refers to a group of therapies that help children recognize their thought patterns and identify where those patterns help and where they hurt. When a child suffers with Obsessive-Compulsive Disorder, the CBT therapy of choice is Exposure Response Prevention (ERP). It helps children face their fears while refraining from compulsive behaviors. Using a graded **stepladder** approach and repeated exposure as part of treatment, the child slowly and systematically faces his fears and reduces the symptoms of his anxiety along with his compulsive behavior.

Obsessive-Compulsive Disorder (OCD)

Children with OCD have unwanted and repeated thoughts and feelings (i.e. obsessions) that drive them to repeat thoughts and/or behaviors over and over which then become compulsive rituals, like washing their hands excessively because of a fear of germs. If the child is unable to complete the ritual, it can cause great distress and anxiety.

In this *I'M AFRAID* book, Khloe Kitten wants to go down a tube slide, like her friends, but she's afraid of germs. To overcome her fear, she uses a stepladder process to gradually expose herself to germs while controlling her obsessive behavior. With patience and courage, Khloe manages her anxiety and reaches her goal.

For more information on Obsessive-Compulsive Disorder, visit:
www.DrMadeleineVieira.com/books/imafraid/obsessive-compulsivedisorder

To check out the other books in the *I'M AFRAID* series, visit:
www.DrMadeleineVieira.com/books/imafraid

About the Author

Dr. Madeleine Vieira is a Clinical Child Psychologist with a special interest in Childhood Anxiety Disorders and Infant Mental Health. She has completed a range of studies to post-doctorate level and is continually expanding her academic and professional development and expertise. She has attended universities in both the United States and United Kingdom, among them are the University of California, Los Angeles and the University of Oxford.

Dr. Vieira has lived in seven countries and currently resides in London, UK with her husband and three children. They have a Shih-Tzu called Caesar who barks too much when the doorbell rings and is nothing like the Emperor! Dr. Vieira's hobbies include, portrait photography, world travels, dancing, and languages.

Working in private practice, Dr. Vieira offers Cognitive Behavioral Therapy (CBT), Cognitive Behavioral Play Therapy, Play and Creative Arts Therapy, and Diagnostic Assessments to children. Along with this, Dr. Vieira offers Clinical Supervision to Play and Creative Arts Therapy trainees and professionals.

In addition to being a registered Clinical Psychologist with the Health and Care Professions Council (HCPC), Dr. Vieira is a qualified Test/Assessment User registered with the British Psychological Society (BPS). She is also an accredited Play and Creative Arts Therapist and Certified Senior Clinical Supervisor in Play and Creative Arts Therapy registered with Play Therapy United Kingdom (PTUK).

To add to her many credentials, Dr. Vieira is Cool Kids accredited by the NSW Education Standards Authority (NESA) which involves treating childhood anxiety through a specifically designed Cognitive Behavioral Therapy (CBT) program of which graded exposure is an essential component.

Specializing in the diagnosis and treatment of Childhood Anxiety Disorders, Dr. Vieira is passionate about alleviating symptoms of children suffering from anxiety. Her *I'M AFRAID* anxiety disorder therapeutic children's series was created out of this passion. Through this series, Dr. Vieira hopes to reach children worldwide, well beyond her practice, as well as have it serve as a therapeutic tool to other mental health professionals.

You can learn more about Dr. Vieira and her practice on her website:
www.DrMadeleineVieira.com

Coping Strategies

1. Tell your parents, teacher, or other person you trust about your fear.

2. Think positive: "I can face this fear and handle uncomfortable feelings."

3. Talk back to your fear: "OCD, I'm in control."

4. Fight fear not just in what you *do*, but with how you *think*. Imagine yourself as a champion fear fighter.

5. Fight OCD by doing the OPPOSITE of what it wants. By going against what the OCD "bully thoughts" are telling you to do, your brain will learn to stop listening to them.

6. Take slow, deep breaths to make you feel calmer.

7. Remind yourself that the anxiety is only temporary; it will not hurt you, and it will pass.

8. Use a stepladder approach to manage your anxiety by taking steps to gradually expose yourself to your biggest fear.

    a. Decide on how many steps you will try to achieve your goal and overcome that biggest fear.

    b. Figure out what each step will be. List and number the steps on a piece of paper before attempting the first step.

    c. Start with small, less difficult steps (bottom of stepladder) and work toward bigger, more challenging ones (top of stepladder) until you reach your main goal.

    d. Before beginning, choose a reward for each step with the last, most challenging step deserving the best reward. Even an attempt that fails deserves a reward for trying.

    e. As you go through your steps, you will have obsessive (uncontrollable) thoughts. Let these thoughts happen while trying to avoid using compulsive (repetitive) behaviors to ease them.

    f. Practice each step several times, and only when you feel comfortable enough with the step, do you move on to the next one.

    g. Continue to use the other coping strategies as you go through each step.

9. It's recommended you seek help from a mental health professional.

Stepladder

Goal Reward

8. Reward

7. Reward

6. Reward

5. Reward

4. Reward

3. Reward

2. Reward

1. Reward

Ingram Content Group UK Ltd.
Milton Keynes UK
UKHW051240160523
421809UK00004B/30